FROM THE LIBRARY OF

Heidi Bensiger
Christmas 1975

She Was Nice To Mice

The Other Side of Elizabeth I's Character Never Before Revealed by Previous Historians

by Alexandra Elizabeth Sheedy
illustrated by Jessica Ann Levy

McGRAW-HILL BOOK COMPANY
New York · St. Louis · San Francisco · Toronto
Mexico · Düsseldorf

Designed by Lynn Braswell

Text copyright © 1975 by Alexandra Elizabeth Sheedy
Illustrations copyright © 1975 by Jessica Ann Levy

3456789RABP798765

Library of Congress Cataloging in Publication Data

Sheedy, Alexandra Elizabeth.
She was nice to mice.

SUMMARY: The memoirs of a literary mouse living
at the court of Elizabeth I reveal the public and
private life of the Queen and her courtiers.
 1. Elizabeth, Queen of England, 1533–1603—Juve-
nile fiction. [1. Elizabeth, Queen of England,
1533–1603—Fiction. 2. Great Britain—History—
Elizabeth, 1558–1603—Fiction. 3. Mice—Fiction]
I. Levy, Jessica Ann. II. Title.
PZ7.S53825Sh   [Fic]   75-9960
ISBN 0-07-056515-5
ISBN 0-07-056516-3 lib. bdg.

Chapter 6 first appeared in the August 1975 issue of Seventeen.

*For Queen Elizabeth I,
without whom this book
could never have been written.*

Chapter
1

*T*HE CITY OF LONDON *is one great maze of streets. Some are noisy, some are quiet, some are rich, and some are poor. Many people from all over the world come to see the Great Tower of London, while Buckingham Palace draws others. Walking along, gazing at beautiful houses and great mansions on streets that still look like long ago, one might think, "What important person could have lived here or there?"*

On one such street, at 189 Plum Pit Grove, a small mouse named Esther Long Whiskers Gray Hair Wallgate the 42nd lived in an eighteenth-century mansion with forty-nine other mouse families. There was something unusual about Esther Long Whiskers

Gray Hair Wallgate the 42nd. She had a history, which is something not all mice have. And, as she herself would say, biting into a bit of cheese on rye and settling back, legs properly crossed, to enjoy her afternoon tea, "Not all mice have literary minds either."

This story is about Esther who not only had a history and a literary mind, but very long whiskers of which she was very proud. It is also about a small woman with a large reputation—Queen Elizabeth I, who has been known to have a certain kind of character.

Esther's house in Wallgate Mansion was right behind the couch in the grand parlor. This was the choicest place for a mouse to live, and Esther had first claim to it because of her history. Her great-great-great-great-great-grandparents had made the original hole there. Right in the best place.

The parlor was ideal for mice because it was the best-cared-for room in Wallgate Mansion, pleasantly warm in winter, pleasantly cool in summer. Esther especially liked the couch because of its plush upholstery. Whenever she needed to cover a chair in her hole, or an extra rug for company, or sometimes a blanket, or something to be made into pillows, a little bit of fabric could be chewed off where it was barely noticeable. Esther would excuse herself for this destruction by saying, "The couch is against the wall. It will never be missed."

Another good thing about the couch was how well it was stationed. One could sneak out of the hole, scamper along under the couch, slide along the floor by the edge of the rug—its gray color being exceedingly useful for camouflage—until reaching the polished wooden table with the round, crystal-clear glass top. The table was excellent for sliding on. It was, in fact, used by the mice as a skating rink in the small hours of the morning. Mr. Small Chair, the husband of Esther's dearest friend, usually danced on the piano keys for delightful music to accompany the gliding.

Mr. and Mrs. Small Chair lived across the parlor from Esther in an antique armchair. This was a popular location, since it was right next to the candy bowl, which had wonderful choices for sweet-toothed mice. Mrs. Small Chair herself was not fond of candy, so there was always a good assortment in the bowl. She usually had a great many visitors. They would enter, stare greedily at the candy, act very polite, have a little chat, exchange gossip, and then casually say, "Ah! Is that one lime? My goodness, I

haven't tasted lime in weeks." Mrs. Small Chair would always insist that Esther take a cream-filled one back to her hole with her.

One of Mrs. Small Chair's frequent visitors was Madame Wimble, who lived behind the draperies. She considered herself, and was considered by others, to be very distinguished because her mother had been the only daughter of a very rich mouse who was also a politician noted for his authority and power. Madame Wimble also often visited Esther and took tea with her because they were of the same class. Almost. Esther, who wanted more than anything to be distinguished, was always trying to make a good impression upon her, so you may well guess where Mrs. Small Chair's candy went when Madame Wimble came. And you can imagine that on these occasions the plush rugs must be put on the floor and the plush pillows on the chairs.

One day when they were having tea, Esther picked up a book and began to read—which might be called bad manners, but which definitely made an impression.

"Esther, darling, I never knew you could read," Madame Wimble said.

"You didn't?" Esther asked, smiling inside.

"No dear, I didn't," Madame Wimble said, wiping her mouth daintily on a little bit of plush.

Esther put down the book and leaned back. "I have a literary mind," she said, twitching her whiskers.

"Indeed? And where did you learn this reading technique?"

"My great-ancestors were very learned. It's a tradition to be smart in my family," Esther said.

"I see, Esther dear. By the way, is that cream-filled?" Madame Wimble pointed to one of Mrs. Small Chair's candies.

"Yes." Esther gazed longingly at it and thought how nice it would be after a hot supper and an evening of skating.

"Esther darling, you wouldn't be so good as to let me have it, would you? For my husband? You know how he loves Mrs. Small Chair's candies."

Esther thought how she loved Mrs. Small Chair's candies, too.

"You can have it," she said reluctantly. One must be kind to guests, she thought. Especially distinguished ones.

"Thank you darling. I do appreciate your generosity. Well, I must be going now. Really, I must." She picked up the candy and left.

Esther wrapped some cotton around her feet and scampered along to the skating rink on the table top. All the mice were there, since the people in the house were now asleep. Here and there in the darkness you could see lights which were mouse lights. They were made from humans' candle grease which the mice stole from candlesticks and made into their own candles.

Mr. Small Chair started to dance on the piano keys and they all began to skate. Esther slid on her cotton-wrapped feet around and around the table top. She was not a very good skater, hard as that was to admit to herself, and she had to shuffle her feet slowly. This evening she watched enviously as Mistress Bright Eyes of Table Drawer did a series of turns right across the table top. Then Sir Wimble slid up to her.

"Thank you very graciously much for the candy. My wife loved it."

"Your wife! Did you not have any?"

"Yes, I did, a taste only. I'm not very fond of sweets."

Imagine! Madame Wimble's deviousness! With these thoughts in her head she suddenly fell on the glass and her skirts whirled about her.

"Esther! Are you all right?" many mice asked.

"Yes, thank you," said Esther primly. A crowd gathered around her and she was feeling properly embarrassed. A pain was starting somewhere in the middle of her tail.

"I'm going," she announced, and swept off holding her tail tightly. When she arrived home she bathed the tail and went to bed thinking how soothing the cream-filled candy would have been just then. She blew out the candle and lay in the dark thinking. She liked to think. A knock was heard on her door.

"Who is it?" she asked.

"It's Mrs. Small Chair."

Esther got out of bed and opened the door.

"Here," Mrs. Small Chair said, and put a candy in Esther's paw. "This will soothe your tail. I really came to tell you that you have mail. It will be delivered to you tomorrow morning. Take care."

"Good night, Mrs. Small Chair." Esther climbed into bed. She loved getting letters. She wondered what it could be.

Chapter
2

*M*OST PEOPLE ARE UNAWARE *that the mouse world is one community—that, in fact, there is even a postal system, the World Wide Mouse-Only Post Delivery. This is the only way mice can communicate with each other from faraway places. If you are a mouse in New York and need to send a letter to London, you merely have it passed along from mouse to mouse until it can be sneaked aboard a boat going to England; the boat mice will make arrangements to have it finally delivered to the house of the addressee. Which is the way Esther received her mail the following morning.*

She was eating her breakfast (cheese bits that she'd melted over a candle flame onto rye crumbs) when a small voice whispered, "Miss Esther?"

"Yes! Yes!" she squeaked and went running to her holestep. A very dusty, tired-looking mouse was practically lying across it. "Do come in!" she said. "Are you all right?" She helped him in, put his mailbag on the floor and gave him some cheese bits, which revived him a little. "Did you have trouble finding me?" she asked.

"Terrible." He licked his paws.

Esther winced. One just did not lick one's paws.

"I've been looking for you since dawn," he said. "I have a letter and package for you from America."

"From America?" said Esther. "America? But I don't know anyone there."

He helped himself to some more cheese bits and licked his paws again. "Well, someone knows you." Digging into his bag, he handed her a white envelope and a brown package. "I have to go now. Thanks for the snack."

"Thank you," Esther said. She waited cordially by the holestep until he was gone, then tore open the envelope. Inside was a photograph of an elegantly dressed mouse and a letter. Esther glanced at the signature—Tabbitha Gray Hair Cheesy the 41st. "Why Gray Hair is a family name!" She then looked at the photograph closely.

The mouse in the photograph really was the picture of elegance. Lace gloves, veiled hat. The dress was in very good taste, Esther thought. So rich! It was frilled and looped and tucked and fell to the floor in so many more folds than Esther's. The mouse was also wearing a pearl necklace and diamond rings. Esther put down the photograph and picked up the letter which read as follows:

Dear Miss Esther:

You have never seen me, but I am Tabbitha Gray Hair Cheesy, your cousin. I live here in America and my mother has just passed away. She is your aunt, you know, dear. She has left me the Gray Hair inheritance which was our grandmother's, then your mother's, then my mother's, and now ours! I have divided it according to our tastes. This package is your portion. I have also provided you with a picture of me so you will know who I am in case the need arises. Happy inheritance.

> *Squeakcerely,*
> *Tabbitha Gray Hair Cheesy the 41st*

Esther read the letter twice. Then she folded it and stuffed it back into the envelope. She picked up

Tabbitha's photograph and studied it. She then walked to her dressing table, sat down, and looked at her face. "Some day I shall go to America." She wiggled her whiskers. "I wonder what's in the package," she thought. Could it be perfume and lacy gloves? Or hats and necklaces and petticoats? Or pantaloons and stockings and shiny, polished shoes and emeralds and diamonds and silver and yards and yards of long, silky dresses?

She grew excited and picked up the package, and sat down on a chair in the drawing room. She weighed it, measuring its weight on her paws. "My goodness, it's heavy! Why, it could be many jewels the ways it feels!" In a sudden rush she tore the brown wrapping paper off it. She looked eagerly at its contents. Her face fell.

Inside was a book bound in purple velvet with gold printing on it so faded it was hard to read. Two dingy gold tassels hung from the cover which was dusty and old. The pages inside were very fragile and crumbly. She dropped it on the table, dismay and sadness rushing through her. She sank into her chair.

Madame Wimble bustled in at that moment. "Esther dear. I have been just waiting to ask you what was in the package."

Esther sighed wearily. "It was nothing worth talking about."

"Why, what's this? A book?"

"Yes, Madame Wimble, That's all it is." (Even mice with literary minds can enjoy diamonds more than books at times.)

"Why, it looks very important to me. Purple velvet and gold tassels are royal marks, you know. In spite of the dust it might be something worth looking into, dear. Well, I must be going now. Ta-ta!" And Madame Wimble bustled out just as she had bustled in.

"Good-bye, Madame Wimble." Esther looked at the book. Then she slowly sat down and disdainfully lifted the dusty cover and began to read:

Chapter
3

*F*OR MANY PEOPLE AND MICE, one of Elizabeth's most distinguishing features was her hair—red as a flame and curled and brushed in such a way that it looked soft as the silk on her petticoats. I, myself, always tried to steal some of that hair to make a nest with. I mean, how many mice have royal hair in their nests—and red, at that. It did cheer it up a bit.

We mice became friends with the Beautiful Nest-Supplier (which is what we sometimes called her after we began using her hair for decoration) in my lifetime. I should explain how that all came about—how it really happened. I remember that quite well. Now let me see, was it in the ballroom or the banquet hall? One must be very accurate about firsts, about beginnings. One might suppose it doesn't matter much, but it does. History writing is as much concerned with *places* as dates and events, not to mention personalities and characters.

Well, it was the banquet hall. In the banquet hall—a huge chamber with a white marble floor (imported from Italy where the best marble comes from) which is freezing to the feet, but all in all a favorite room because of the food served in it—we often gathered during feasts and that is where it happened, that is where we became friends with the Queen. Her last name was Elizabeth and on this delicious piece of parchment I stole from her desk it said *Reg*, which was most likely a code name that all royal people used. At any rate—ah yes, I must tell you about her desk. It was messy. Yet it was a rich looking piece of royal furniture and it contained a delicious assortment of documents and parchments that were *magnifique*! (Important mice, cultured mice, speak French.) I could go on and on about her desk and room, but I have a story to tell.

The Queen was having a banquet on this day.

We lord and lady mice were gathered at the entrance to our passages that go all over the palace and occasionally branch off to rooms and royal apartments. In those branch-offs were our homes. My home was called the Branch of the Bedroom and it led right to Her Bedroom.

Well, they were having pudding. Now, Skidmore, my best friend, loves pudding and we could see him practically outside the hole waiting for a bit to drop, as it usually did. Royal people have manners, but they also have accidents. I called to Skidmore, and so did some of the other mice, but *he* wouldn't listen. His eyes were on one man who was gay and young and was chattering away to a lovely girl who had a beautiful face as precise and pale as the Queen's. I later knew her to be the Queen's niece, Arabella Stuart, who always smiled and never screamed when she saw us. Anyway, this man was trying so hard to win the girl's favor that he wasn't paying attention to his eating skills and he began dropping food. He scooped some pudding up on his spoon and, gesturing with great noble strokes, he started showing the girl the correct way to ride a horse.

And then it happened. He had just begun to trot when his spoon of pudding slipped out of his hand and the mushy food plopped straight onto the girl's silken-covered lap. His face turned properly red and he pulled out his white napkin and began to wipe the pudding off. Then Arabella stood up and the bit that was left on her gown fell to the floor, whereupon Skidmore darted out, eager for his share.

As soon as he was noticed the place was in an uproar. Some gallant dukes strode up and,

moving Arabella to one side, tried to trap
Skidmore. All of the noblewomen went quickly,
as one body, to the other side of the hall. The
Queen went straight to her throne. The men
went—as many as a couple hundred of them—
around and around the hall, trying to catch and
undoubtedly kill one small mouse. So much
furor, just to please the Queen! (They thought!)

Skidmore was frantic. He left his pudding and
tried to get away with his life still in him.
"Skidmore! Skidmore!" we all cried.

Skidmore slid under a table, skidded around a
chair and knocked over plates and goblets as he
tried wrapping himself in the tablecloth.

That was where they got him. They unwound
him from the cloth and dragged him to the
middle of the room. Many heads craned forward. And then the worst happened. Some
lords pinned Skidmore down with their feet and
one man came forward with a knife. Skidmore
squeaked and the man shrilled, "Now you little
foul rodent, we'll see your bewitched head roll!
Just like the bewitched Anne Boleyn's did!
Cruel and filthy beings do not live long!" He
raised his hand that held the knife.

"WHAT? STOP IT! STOP IT AT ONCE!"
We all turned our heads. The Queen was standing looking outraged.

"HOW DARE YOU! YOU INSOLENT
FOOL! YOU IDIOTIC TRAITOR! WHAT
WAS THAT YOU SAID ABOUT
MY MOTHER? OR DID YOU NOT
KNOW THAT QUEEN ANNE WAS *MY
MOTHER*?"

"Y-your Most Noble Highness I . . ."

"YOU WHAT?" She crossed to him with
her cheeks aflame. "YOU WHAT?" She began
to shake him. Then she threw him on the floor.
"ON YOUR KNEES, YOU DIRTY, SINFUL
MAN! YOU WHAT? YOU WHAT?"

"I did not mean it Your Most Gracious
Majesty, it just came out."

"YOU FILTHY BEAST, YOU LIAR!"

"But I forgot she was your mother."

"WHAT? DO YOU KNOW HOW
GUILTY YOU ARE MAKING YOURSELF?
ANNE BOLEYN YOU SAID WAS BE-
WITCHED! JUST WHO DID YOU THINK
SHE WAS? I KNOW HOW DISGUSTING
YOU TOADIES ARE! LIARS! SINFUL PEO-

PLE! NOT EVEN PEOPLE—PIGS! HOGS!"

She threw a goblet at him. It landed with a great noise at his feet. "YOU DISGRACEFUL TRAITOR!" She picked up his knife. "Nasty men do not live long," she said quietly.

"TAKE HIM AWAY! TO THE TOWER! WALK HIM THROUGH TRAITOR'S GATE TIME AND TIME AGAIN! TAKE AWAY HIS MONEY, AND HIS LAND! UTTERLY DISGRACE HIM! GET HIM OUT OF MY SIGHT!"

She turned to the men who had trapped Skidmore. "Get your feet off him! Poor little pest. Feed him. Give him some pudding. He has just done me a favor." The Queen held out some pudding to Skidmore. Skidmore took it and licked her hand.

The Queen gave Skidmore a little push. Then she saw us. "Ah, so you have friends and family," she said. "More pudding. Or is there not some cheese? Here, my friends." She picked up some scraps from the table and scattered them about the room, calling to us to come and eat. Then she turned to the guests and said, "Well, don't just stand there. You came for a banquet. SO BANQUET!''

Long after the banquet had ended and the lords and ladies had gone to their chambers, Elizabeth sat on her throne just looking at the knife and the hole from which we came and went. Then she said softly, ''Mother. My dear mother. How I love you and miss you.''

During the years we knew her she often said that to herself, but she would never let any of her courtiers hear her saying those words. Elizabeth had a public and a private self. We often observed her in public and she was very different indeed from the person we knew privately.

Chapter
4

*I*N THOSE DAYS THE PALACE was full of lights
and sounds. This was due to the fact that it
was always full of parties. Our Queen loved
parties and clothes and jewels and dancing,
which she encouraged plenty of at her very
frequent banquets. She also enjoyed singling
out favorite lords and ladies to honor, thereby
making everyone else jealous. She was quite
shrewd about people and their feelings, and
because she was contemptuous of their flattery
she would sometimes play one off against the
other.

When Elizabeth picked a favorite, we mice
were among the first to know. She would have
certain favorites one year, and different ones the

next. But two who were always her favorites were Sir Walter Raleigh and the Earl of Essex. Especially Essex. He was always the first picked to dance, ride, eat, and even sleep with her.

And then one night, a beautiful night, a very English night all soft with stars, Essex met Arabella Stuart. It was at a ball where Arabella was first introduced to many of Elizabeth's favorites. Essex was there, gay and laughing with the charm yet dignity that had captured Elizabeth's glance and held it, but when Elizabeth introduced him to her niece Arabella, Essex was the one who was charmed.

Arabella was so delicate and pretty, with hands as white and soft as Elizabeth's. One's hands were an attraction. Essex sat by Arabella at the table and kept her listening to his enchanting stories and witty jokes. Elizabeth noticed this and was not so pleased, but remarked to Arabella, "He has a liking for you, does he not?"

In our mouse holes we, too, were having a party, for my aunt was to be wed. But I enjoyed sneaking away to watch and observe the more exciting world outside our homes. I am very clever. I always could tell just what our Queen was thinking, even though she never showed it by her expression. Although none of the other people at the banquet could tell how angry the Queen was at the way Essex was paying attention to Arabella, I knew and longed to run out on that freezing floor and comfort her and tell her it was all right. (But, as it turned out, I was wrong about that.)

The dancing started and the courtiers promenaded through the hall. Arabella did not know how this was done, so she sat on a silken couch. Elizabeth was sitting on her throne watching the dancers and Essex was dancing with one of the ladies-in-waiting. Arabella watched everything and everyone, but she seemed to be unhappy. The Queen then left her throne and was talking with a duke. As the music ended and another dance was struck up, Essex went to Arabella and offered her his arm. Arabella shook her head. This dance too was one she apparently did not know and in a few minutes I saw Arabella and Essex going off into the adjoining room.

Quickly I scurried down a passage and found a hole to look through. The music could plainly be heard from the banquet hall and Essex was teaching Arabella that dance and the next one and soon Arabella was whirling and turning and her silk slippers flashed by my hole every minute.

And all the time I thought of the Queen. What would she do? Her anger when aroused was great. She had been known to have someone killed for an insult. And here was the one man she loved, charmed by her own niece. I feared her tricky ways, yet Queen could be kind. She had saved Skidmore, she fed us frequently, and she was also playful with us. But this might be different.

Now music was coming through the hall. Arabella knew the dance and Essex danced close to her and lightly squeezed her hand.

"You're a very good teacher," said Arabella shyly.

"Am I now?" said Essex delightedly. "Or maybe you are a good learner." He stopped her and took her hand in his.

"I don't think you should take my hand like that," said Arabella, again shyly, giving him a side glance that plainly said she wasn't joking.

"Why not?" And Essex gazed into her eyes. I watched with my heart beating very fast. Essex said, "The Queen? Is that it?" Arabella nodded.

"Nonsense," said Essex. "Why should she care?" And he picked up Arabella's hand and kissed it.

"I DO CARE." The voice that said these words was icy. "I CARE WHEN YOU FROL-IC OFF AND DO NOT ATTEND MY BAN-QUETS." Queen looked at Essex's lips frozen to Arabella's hand. "TAKE YOUR MOUTH OFF THAT GIRL'S HAND!"

Essex obeyed.

"I WOULD LIKE TO KNOW WHAT YOU HAVE BEEN DOING HERE!"

"Your Majesty's niece did not know the dance and I set it upon me to teach her," said Essex with a bow.

"I WAS VERY MUCH AWARE OF THAT, ESSEX. SO KEEP FLOURISHES FOR MORE APPROPRIATE TIMES WHEN YOU CAN INFORM ME. But, My Lord," she said sarcastically, "does hand kissing come as part of the dance? Inform me of this."

"It was merely a kind gesture and welcome," said Essex boldly.

"Too kind, perhaps." And Queen smiled. Only I knew what that smile meant. "Well, Essex?" she said, and stopped and waited.

Essex looked questioningly at her. She waited deliberately. It was a terrible silence—the Queen trying to hold back anger and jealousy in front of Arabella, and Essex being only too aware of it.

Finally, Essex spoke. "Shall we return to the banquet?" he ventured.

"To whom are you speaking?" Elizabeth asked cleverly, waiting to explode.

Essex looked from one to the other.

Then Arabella spoke shyly, eying the Queen. "If it please Your Majesty, I will retire," she said.

"Yes, my dear. I am afraid the strain of the Court was too much for you today. So . . ." The Queen looked meanly at them. "MAYBE YOU SHOULD NOT RETURN FOR A FEW WEEKS. YOU NEED A REST."

"Yes, Your Grace." Arabella curtsied and hastily left.

"I will see you as soon as my anger has subsided, Essex. IF IT DOES." And Elizabeth swept out of the room.

Chapter 5

I KNEW THAT QUEEN would go and retire and I found different passages to get to her chambers. She had a small waiting room in front of her boudoir and here I hid under a chair and waited. Queen entered in her full Court attire and sat down at her writing table. Her maidens, under royal command, scurried into Queen's boudoir to prepare it for her retirement. Elizabeth seemed tired as she picked up a scroll to read. One could see she was waiting for Essex.

But when he knocked and entered the room she didn't so much as look up, and because she didn't want to seem to be waiting for him she kept the parchment up to her face. I saw her glance at an elaborate clock once or twice and surely she must have read that document three or four times before she even looked up. She left him standing there waiting to be recognized. Finally she said calmly, "Sit down."

Essex did so, eying the Queen carefully.

"I have things to discuss with you, Essex." She then examined her rings and jewelry for a long time before she spoke.

"I am very much annoyed with you." Here she stopped.

Essex, looking uncomfortable, cleared his throat and ventured, "Yes Your Grace?"

"Arabella Stuart is my niece. She came here on a visit. TOO BAD IT HAS TO BE SO SHORT. Arabella Stuart came here on my pleasure, not on *yours*!"

"Your Grace, I—"

Queen held up her hand. "YOU WILL WAIT!"

Essex looked intently at Queen's face. "Do not be—be jealous," he said slowly.

"HOW DARE YOU COME IN HERE AND SAY SUCH A THING! ESSEX, YOU ARE A FOOL! DO YOU NOT KNOW THE

LIMITS OF ANGER? THERE ARE NONE!"
She looked defiantly at him. "YOU WILL
LEAVE THIS ROOM AT ONCE! GO!" She
pointed a long white finger. "OUT!"

I trembled beneath my chair.

Essex looked at her blankly, then abruptly
stood up and walked quickly to the door.

"WAIT!" Elizabeth rose and took a step
toward him. His back was toward her. "Where
are you going?" she asked a bit too quietly.

Essex turned swiftly and said softly, "To
someone who needs me."

"AND WHO, MAY I ASK, MIGHT
THAT BE?"

"Lady Arabella Stuart. Who do you think? I
go where I am wanted, which is certainly not
here." He bowed saucily and left, slamming the
door behind him. All was quiet.

The Queen advanced to the door. She stuck
her fiery red head, adorned with the pearls and
diamonds of the Court, out into the passageway.
"ESSEX! ESSEX!" she screamed in a terrible
voice. Essex stopped at once in his angry walk
toward the stairs at the end of the hall. Queen
did not go toward him. She remained at the
door.

I viewed all of this from the hall, for by this time I had scudded out from under the chair and was hiding in the shadows of the flickering torches to see this scene more clearly.

Then Queen spoke quietly. "You will return to your own chamber. Miss Arabella Stuart has company enough in her chamber. Good night, Essex." And I just had time to scurry into the room before she slammed her door.

Queen stood silent for a moment inside her waiting room before entering her boudoir. Then she called to her maidens, who responded at once. "I am going to take a walk," she announced, "out to the gardens to enjoy the fresh night air."

"Yes, Your Grace," and "Yes, Milady," they responded at once, and "Do you need an escort, Your Grace?"

But Elizabeth did not want an escort and she put on her cloak and left her chambers. The maidens left soon after to return to their quarters until Queen came back. I waited a while and then sneaked into Queen's boudoir.

On her vanity table was a silver hairbrush which I spied, and wrapped around the bristles were some wisps of beautiful red curls. I made my way up to the top of the table and pulled some off with my teeth. They were soft and I supposed they would make a good bed.

Then I heard someone in the room outside Queen's boudoir. Thinking it was a handmaiden, I hid behind a large jewelry box. Peeping around it, I saw a man walking into the room. It was Essex! I squeaked. If Queen found him her anger would be great and I feared it, not for myself, but for it alone, and for Essex. Essex looked scared too, but determined.

Then I heard footsteps outside, and Essex heard them too, because he stopped and stood very still. The door creaked. "It's the Queen's maidens," he said softly to himself, but worriedly. And then he rushed into Queen's boudoir, got down on the floor, and crawled under the royal bed. And just in time—for in came not the maidens but Queen herself and she looked suspiciously around the room.

By this time I had come out from behind the box and was standing up on my hind legs with my front paws resting on the rim of a small bowl filled with perfumed water. Unfortunately, in my eagerness to see what the Queen was doing I leaned over and fell in with a splash and some squeaks.

Elizabeth turned quickly toward me. "So it is *you* making such a racket," she exclaimed and scooped me out of the bowl. She lifted the hem of her silken dress, dried me, and then rubbed me against her chalked cheek, saying, "So you thought you'd have a bath, eh."

In the mirror I saw Essex putting one hand forth from under the bed in an effort to get out. I tensed up.

Elizabeth said, "You do not like to be held and caressed?" in a good-natured way.

Just then her maidens came in and she put me down. Essex quickly withdrew his parts which were now showing. I was so relieved that I squeaked with delight. The maidens seated Queen and proceeded to get her ready for her bed. The thought of Essex under the bed was so

funny that I rolled over and over. I then watched with great interest, and only a few chuckles, what happened next.

First, Queen's cloak was removed. Then her overdress of silver and gold and velvet and silk that shimmered and shone was taken off. It was a Court dress and looked exceedingly beautiful on Queen. Next came her underdress of silvery cloth that shone, too, and had a huge ruffle along the bottom which formed the hem. This ruffle showed from under the Court dress and made it look very fancy indeed. Underneath this was yet another underwear-type dress of dazzling white silk with lace and a sprinkling of shiny stones that I think might have been diamonds on the edges. It had a thick petticoat skirt. Under this was an under-type shirt with full sleeves and a low square neck. Her bosoms were arranged in such a way that they formed a gentle mound just curving above the top of the shirt. Elizabeth, to my taste, was a beauty. Under the first petticoat was a second. And a third and a fourth. Queen wore many petticoats to make her dresses very full and wide, as was the style. When these were removed she was in her underwear. Even that was fancy, too. The shirt top and skirt were thin and gauzy and around the middle of her body was a tightening device which, in fact, was responsible for pushing up her bosoms. This was removed, too. Then the maidens wrapped Elizabeth in a silken robe and she seated herself in front of her mirror. I suspected Essex was witnessing all of this undressing from his hiding place under the bed.

Then Queen removed her gleaming headpiece. And then—did I not tell you—her wig. Queen had no hair. She wore many beautifully styled wigs. Now she put on a light little one to sleep in, since, just in case someone came in at night, she would not like to be seen without any hair. Then she removed her grease paint which really was grease, and her white makeup that she wore which was really a chalk substance. It was thickly applied to her skin, and on it she would darken her brows. Actually she drew them on because she hadn't any, and she drew them so they were thin and black, and she would draw a line around her eyes, too. But now, however, she was taking all of it off, even her red lip paint.

Then she had her shoes removed and her handmaidens left her as she dismissed them. Queen picked up her silver hairbrush. She looked very different without her makeup and state wig. Queen brushed her Court wig very nicely so it shone and it looked like real hair. Then she got up and crossed the room to her wardrobe.

It was then that Essex scrambled out from underneath the bed.

Queen turned and put her hand up to her mouth in shock. "ESSEX!" she gasped. "ESSEX! WHAT ARE YOU DOING UNDER MY BED?"

Essex stood up and smiled. "How long you've been. Women take so long to prepare and unprepare."

"YOU SAW!" Queen stared stonily at him. "I am very much annoyed with you, Essex," she said.

Essex bowed deeply. "I *saw* nothing. I merely waited, and it was very uncomfortable under that bed." And then he looked up and gazed at her closely and intently. "Your face . . ." he said.

"SAVE YOUR COMMENTS, ESSEX," she hissed angrily. "STATE YOUR BUSINESS HERE AND GET OUT BEFORE I KICK YOU!"

"Your Grace, I wanted to beg your forgiveness. I am your favorite. And you are my favorite. You are a beautiful woman and I am proud to be your favorite, so please let us keep it that way. I was wrong to pay so much attention to Lady Arabella. I want to be with you. I wish to stay here." Essex picked up her hand. He kissed it. Then he held it in both his hands.

Queen withdrew from him. "Do you really mean that, Essex? Or is it an act? I know how you are with women."

"I really mean it," Essex said.

"Well, Essex," said the Queen, "I was just retiring."

Essex looked crestfallen.

"Come," she said and took his hand and kissed it! And then *she* embraced *him*. She led him to the bed smiling. Elizabeth gracefully sank onto the silken cover.

Essex sat on the edge and took his boots, jacket, shirt, and stockings off. He stood up and

removed his pants and was there in his underwear. Then he turned, and went about the room
blowing out the candles.

It was very dark now and I couldn't see
anything. But I heard.

Elizabeth said to him, "You have a strong
body, my love."

And Essex said, "Have I, now? You really
think so?"

I was beginning to feel
uncomfortable. I thought
they should have some
privacy. So I made my
way down the dressing
table and carefully found
my way out of the bou-
doir. I slipped along the

hall back to my hole where I myself went to bed,
alone. I fell asleep thinking about Elizabeth and
Essex together, what I had witnessed and what
was right now taking place!

Chapter 6

I WAS LYING IN BLANKETS on the floor of my house a few miserable rainy days after Elizabeth and Essex worked out their problems about Arabella Stuart. Elizabeth had sent her from the Court, and Essex, although a bit soured by this, was still just as entertaining and pleasant to the Queen in her presence. I only saw Essex around the Queen, but Skidmore had reported to me that he had seen Essex moping around in his chamber and heard him mumbling about the Queen's jealousy. So I was curled up in my blankets thinking about how complicated it must be to be in love, when Skidmore skidded in, landing in a small clump of excitement by my fire.

"Well, bless my whiskers, Skidmore!" I exclaimed in delight. "Skidmore, I'm so happy to see you, I'm *so* hungry for news and company. You're soothing to my sore throat and pleasant to my stuffed head. I have been simply miserable with a cold these past few days, miserably sick, and miserably lonely. So stay awhile and tell me the news."

Skidmore sniffed and said, "Can't stay. Have to alert the rest of the families, because we're going to have a great entertainment tonight and I hope you'll be well enough to come. Guess who's coming? Your favorite, *Shakespeare!*" With that, he was out of the hole.

Skidmore really was my friend. Shakespeare was my favorite and I wouldn't have wanted to miss seeing him even once, and feeling as I did I certainly would not have ventured out that miserable, damp and chilly night for any other reason. To my taste Shakespeare was almost as fascinating as the Queen. He was a playwright. Comedies, histories, happy silly plays, mystical magical plays all flowed forth from his quill, even tragedies. He would write a new one, bring it to the Court, and act it out, playing every part himself.

When I was very young, my mother would take me to see him and so he became important to me at any early age. Nobody else who came to Court to entertain could ever match him. Queen enjoyed Shakespeare, too, more than anyone knew, except we small ones who were able to see behind her fan, which she usually held up to her face. I saw her wipe away many a sad tear and have many a good laugh at his entertainments.

Forgetting my cough and headache and sniffly nose, I hurried to the throne room. The crowd filled the elegant hall. It was all glowing from candles, and light was reflected from the jewels the women were wearing and shimmering with glimmers from the shiny gold threads embroidered on the clothing. I climbed to the top of the throne by digging my pawnails into the spaces in the carving on the back. When Queen entered, followed by Essex, I knew it was almost time.

Elizabeth was dressed in silk—white silk embroidered with gold and silver threads and glittering with diamonds. Her ruffled lace collar rose high around her face and her brilliant red hair was curled and covered by a scattering of diamonds. Queen walked regally to her chair and sat down, looking expectantly toward the grand doors.

Essex approached her. "Ah, Your Grace," he said flatteringly. "How goest all with thou?" And he laughed at his formal speech, I think, probably because he had just been with her privately. The laugh was high and loud and humorous and it caught the attention of everyone who looked at Essex's splendid face and golden beard and hair framing it.

The Queen smiled an enchanting smile. "You do not fool me, Essex!" And then she whispered, "You know well what I have been doing."

I wanted to know as well as the others who heard the whisper, and I dratted my cold which had kept me away from the Queen's chambers.

Then, suddenly, the doors opened and in came a man. That man. The man Shakespeare. A most noble looking one—with a pointy beard and a soft mustache. He was dressed in velvet—green velvet and white lace. A servant attending him brought various papers and laid them on a table. Shakespeare walked forward to the throne and knelt.

Elizabeth proudly smiled down at him and held out her hand. "Shakespeare," she said.

Shakespeare kissed her hand and looked at

the Queen's face. Then he said, "It's a tragedy today, Your Grace, from the chronicles of our history. It is not yet finished, I think, but I will try it out."

There was one thing about Shakespeare that

was not so entertaining. His speeches. He always made speeches before he performed. I believe he wrote as many speeches as he wrote plays, and often they were almost as long and one could get very bored and wish he would get on with his entertainment. So I settled myself down anticipating a long wait.

Some time into the speech Skidmore scurried up the throne to me exclaiming, *"C'est drôle, c'est drôle!"* which means in French something's hilarious.

"What's *drôle*, Skidmore?" I squeaked softly.

Skidmore pointed toward the table where the papers were that Shakespeare's servant had brought in. I looked and saw about a dozen tiny mice tearing the pages to shreds and eating them as fast as they tore them.

Now, as I mentioned before, I love the plays and this was too much for me because I thought those mice might be ruining my evening. The only thing for us to do was to stop them. But, if we ventured across the floor we might be caught. The Queen was so absorbed in Shakespeare that she didn't notice what was going on at the table. And knowing she would be angry when she found out, too, I decided to warn her.

I pawed my way through her collar to her ear and gave it a nip.

The Queen jumped, and as I was trying to keep my balance I got my paw caught in her large diamond earring. It pulled on her ear and she gave a loud cry and pulled me off by the tail.

Shakespeare had not noticed and was still droning on with his speech. His eyes were on the ceiling and his hands stretched out toward the Queen. Queen was trying to listen and at the same time I was trying to point out the shredding mice while Skidmore was making a racket behind us laughing and squeaking. I wiggled in the air and the Queen gave me a shake.

"What is wrong?" she asked angrily. "You mice stop bothering and pestering me!"

It was then that she saw the other mice eating the play as fast as they could. She gasped and cried, "ESSEX, THOSE MONSTERS ARE EATING THE PLAY! STOP THEM AT ONCE!" and she dropped me to the floor.

I ran to stop my friends. Knowing Elizabeth was watching me, I scurried up the table as fast as I could and bit them and clawed them away from the papers and then chased them off the table.

Shakespeare turned then and said sharply, "Stop that racket! Can't you see I am entertaining Her Majesty?" But Queen was already rustling across the room and she pulled the sheets away from the mice and gathered them up.

She was so annoyed at the mess and the noise that she threw me off the table to the floor, forgetting it was I who had helped her. My head hit the floor and I became enveloped in dizzy darkness. When I next became aware of what was going on around me, I found I was lying on Queen's lap and her soft fingers were stroking me. I was so happy I nipped at her fingers.

Shakespeare was standing in front of us with the rescued pages of his play. This one was all about a wicked lord of olden times who, with the help of his evilly clever wife, murdered his king and took his throne. Shakespeare, just as he usually did, was acting all the parts, and beautifully, too. With no costumes and no scenery it is often hard to make a play seem real, yet he did it. First he entered as the lord; next he became the three strange witches who told him his fate. He had a way of becoming everyone at once, moving from character and part to character and part with perfect ease.

It was a long and sad play, but I loved it—especially when the lord's wife went mad and walked around with a dagger in her hand, thrusting it into pillows and tapestries. Queen loved it too. At the end, when the lord and his wife are dead because of their treasonous deeds, she applauded loudly, as did the rest of the audience. She also hit the arm of her throne several times, saying, "HEAR! HEAR!" You could tell the ending suited her.

Afterward we all adjourned to the banquet hall where a feast was laid out. But to tell you the truth it reminded me of a gory banquet scene in the play and so I completely lost my appetite. No one else seemed to have lost theirs and they fell to the roasted joints hungrily. As for me and Skidmore, we decided to return to my hole for a soothing cup of tea.

We talked for a few hours and if I had not been sick I would have paid a visit to the Queen's chambers. But Skidmore went instead for me. I couldn't wait for the next day. Skidmore had promised to come for breakfast.

Chapter
7

SKIDMORE DRAINED the last drop of tea from his cup. "Well, Skidmore," I said. "What happened last night?"

Skidmore blinked at me, then winked. "Last night? Ah yes, *last night*," he said. "Not much. Queen went to bed and Essex talked with her awhile and then he slept with her, I guess."

"What do you mean, *you guess*, Skidmore?" I asked. "Didn't you see?"

"Oh no," Skidmore said, "I was too embarrassed to look."

"Oh Skidmore," I sighed, "you're not much of an envoy. What am I going to do with you?"

"Well, you can give me some more tea," he said. We both laughed.

All of a sudden Sir Wilkin of Stone Corner, which is, in fact, right near the pantry of the royal kitchen, scooted in. We both stood up.

"Sir?" I said.

Sir Wilkin waddled over and flopped down to catch his breath. "Dear gentlemice," he said, "I have such news as you have never imagined."

"What is it?" Skidmore and I craned our necks forward.

"The ratcatcher is coming tomorrow."

We were all silent for a moment, as we looked at each other in dismay. Then, seriously, I asked, "What should we do?" Our usual hiding place had been covered over with marble.

"Let's hold a meeting," Skidmore suggested. And so we did. And all the mice came to hear Sir Wilkin talk.

After he finished, we decided that our only hope was the Queen. Queen had ordered the catcher. Somehow she should save us. So we held another meeting about the Queen and it was decided that one mouse would be selected to find a way with her.

I knew that I should be the one because I

knew Queen best and she knew me. But the other mice picked Skidmore. Well, I had a little talk with him. At first he was so overwhelmed that he was chosen that he puffed out his little chest and strutted, not listening to a word I said. But finally, he came down to reasoning. Besides, Skidmore was a little afraid of Queen. Therefore, he consented to me being the one.

I went to Queen's chamber that night and waited for her. Once again I watched her undress and then, all of a sudden, I was struck with an idea. A fabulous, marvelous idea. It was brilliant, ingenious. It came when I watched Queen take off all her petticoats. There were so many that when she walked her skirt would

balloon out very far. No one could see under. The mice could hide underneath and walk with her. After all, the Queen wanted to catch rats. Not mice. But how to tell her?

I decided upon the only thing. To fall back into the perfumed water—to catch her attention. And then I could tell her—act it out. Well, I fell into the water and Queen picked me out saying, "You again? Well, I shall have to give you a bath in it. You seem forever to be trying to get clean."

At that moment Essex walked in. "Your Grace, I want to—" and seeing me, said, "Too bad the ratcatcher will get the little beast. It's rather cute." And saved me from having to tell

her. Of course, this set off an explosion of anger from Elizabeth.

"WHAT DO YOU THINK I AM— CRUEL? I ORDERED A *RAT*CATCHER NOT A *MOUSE* ONE!"

Then I jumped out of her hands and scurried under her petticoats. (She was not fully undressed.)

"Where could it have gone?" asked Queen, who had not seen me run to my hiding place. I scratched her leg and she lifted her petticoats to look at me. Then she gave a little push with her foot and I went running off to tell the others of my idea.

Working together, we all decided on a plan. I told them that Queen would be happy to hide them. So on the appointed hour that the rat-catcher was due, we all sneaked out and in a mass—males, females, and children—we scampered through the halls of the castle and arrived at the Queen's study before the catcher got there.

She was in blue and white, all aglow and glittering. Her pearls shone in her bright hair and she looked so beautiful that we all stopped

together for a moment. Then we marched right
to the ruffle of her gown and slipped under it.

Elizabeth jumped. She looked down. "Why
you sly little things!" she said with pleasure.
"You knew the catcher was coming today," she
laughed. "Very well," she said and lifted her
skirts so that it was easier for us, and then she
dropped them and straightened them around us.

When she walked, we scurried along underneath the gown. It was hot and scratchy underneath and we kept rubbing against those stud-
ded shoes of hers. But it wasn't so bad when we
thought what would happen if we were out in
the open with the rats.

I heard the Queen talking to a lord. And then
she sat down and we peeked out from under that
scratchy skirt and saw that we were in the throne
room and a man was being shown in. He was
dressed shabbily but looked as if what he was
wearing was good enough for him.

Queen said, "Well, if you will proceed with your job and do it well you will be handsomely rewarded. So leave and you may go in every room without permission but with Lord Williams to guide you. Be off!"

The lord and the catcher both knelt together. One jerkily and one smoothly. And then they both departed.

"Well, my little friends, you may play." And she lifted her skirts and we all ran out. We explored the room, sampled everything, until Queen's sharp voice would shoo us away from a pile of papers or a silk-covered chair which looked richly juicy. We climbed over wood carvings and scratched silken screens while Queen sat and seemed to be thinking.

Essex entered the room. "You called for me, Your Grace?"

"Yes, Essex. I wanted to speak with you," Elizabeth sighed. "I am asking Arabella back to Court."

"Back, Your Grace?"

"Mmmmm-hmmmm."

"Why, Your Grace?"

"I need another lady-in-waiting and she is my

niece and a very stately girl, too. I need a young girl around."

Essex stood there and suddenly smiled brightly. "Merry Christmas, Your Grace."

Christmas at Queen Elizabeth's Court was so very festive and frivolous that I have often wondered if any other equaled it. For twelve days straight, starting on Christmas Eve, there were parties and banquets, plays and shows, musicians and jugglers and gymnasts, poets, singers, and many, many, traveling minstrels. Each night the castle was a noisy wonderful sight from the outside, for it was completely lighted and filled with laughter, song, and gaiety, from the tower to the drawbridge.

Many times we mice would sit under the table and watch these parties. We would eat a lot of scraps, enough to "burst your belly," as Skidmore would say. I remember a particularly nice feast which I should like to tell you of. The table was set with an embroidered linen cloth, napkins beside gilded plates and silver bowls with spoons and knives beside them. When the guests had assembled, a toast was made and two large goblets passed from one lord to the other. One goblet started from one end of the table and another goblet from the other until both were handed to one lord at once. He looked at them and then took one and gulped and took the other and had a long draught. This brought a general burst of laughter from the other guests, but not from the Queen.

She was eying Essex who sat not far from her and was talking animatedly and gaily to Arabella Stuart who, of course, on the Queen's wishes had returned. Any fool at that moment could tell he loved her. And Queen was no fool. But I turned my eyes away, for the soups were coming.

There was a dorry onion soup with almonds. *Dorry* means gilded. It had that gilded look to its surface, but the gilt was really almond milk that looked glisteny. There was also an oyster broth followed by lobster and rice and mussels in broth. There was roast goose and peacock and

little pheasants and partridges with raisin stuffing. Then there were spiced pears, wine custard, and plenty of fruit pudding with almond milk.

Then there were little fruitcakes and one had a bean in it. The one who got the bean was to be king or queen of the party for the evening. Elizabeth loved this, for the rivalry for her commanding position even for just a few hours was great. The lord who had all the wine in both goblets got the bean, too. How he laughed! And then all the guests fell to finishing the cakes.

As all of these dishes came and went, we mice got enough scraps to satisfy us for weeks. Then after some more wine, entertainment was introduced. There was a poet and some jugglers. But my favorites were the acrobats. How they flipped and moved! Why, Skidmore was thumping his feet on the floor when they were finished! There was also a group singing.

Afterward, when everyone had left, I spotted Arabella and Essex walking across the empty hall. "Why must she be so jealous?" Essex was saying.

"Oh, but My Lord, you must remember that I have come only as a lady-in-waiting. She can send me home any time she likes."

"Arabella, I—I love—"

"Shhh! You must not say it. You must keep quiet. And keep your feelings to yourself."

They walked on, Arabella's slim, elegant figure with Essex's regal, handsome one. How nice it would be if they could remain happy. But Queen would never have allowed it. They were not even permitted to love. I pitied them.

They reached the end of the hall and Arabella turned. "I must leave now, Essex. My chambers are down that way. You must not be found there. Good-night."

"Good-night." Essex leaned over to kiss her.

"No, you must not! Good-night, Essex."

"Good-night, my love."

Essex turned and started to walk up the length of the hall again. Arabella had already vanished into the shadows.

A few days later Arabella vanished from the Court. Queen simply said, "Christmas is over. You may return home now." She did not even permit Essex to say good-bye.

Chapter
8

ONE DAY AFTER A FEW WEEKS had passed,
I was scampering down a marble staircase
on my way to the banquet hall when I saw Essex
coming toward me with a group of his friends.
One of them remarked, "How happy and gay
Her Majesty seems, now that Lady Arabella is
gone." He said it spitefully. I was amazed that
he could speak so dangerously in front of Essex.

But what Essex said surprised me even more.
He glanced in the lord's direction and said
slowly, "I have the Queen eating out of my
hand. When I am King and rule the country, she
will have to restrain herself because then I will
be the one in power."

"Too bad you're not King now, with this war going on in Ireland. Women cannot manage such things."

I was so shaken by this conversation that I rushed away wishing I had not heard it.

As the rebellion spread in Ireland, the palace became very dull. There were no more parties or banquets because there was no time for them and all of the money had to be used in war. All that took place were meetings and consultations where there was never any food worth stealing.

And then Queen decided to have a private meeting away from the palace with one of her councillors. Essex of course was to come along as well. Since I was longing for adventure, I decided to go with them.

I climbed into the saddlebag that was to be strapped to Queen's white horse. Inside it was full of crumply, uncomfortable papers. The smell of leather was overpowering. When Queen mounted and the horse began to walk, I crawled into a scroll. When the horse began to trot, I was jiggled so much that I began to wish I had stayed home in my hole drinking tea with Skidmore. Just as I was getting horsesick, the horse stopped to my great relief, and I poked my head out for a breath of fresh air. Across a green field, I saw the councillor galloping toward us. As soon as he came up and the conversation began, I realized I was present at a highly important meeting.

Queen was trying to decide which of her lords to send to Ireland to command the troops. It must be someone loyal, brave, trustworthy, and daring. Essex, thinking he could manage Queen, told her to send a man named Carew who was none of these.

Queen cleverly looked him in the eye and said, "It is not your place, Essex, to tell me who to send and who not to. SO KEEP YOUR MOUTH SHUT AND YOUR EARS OPEN AND PERHAPS YOU WILL LEARN SOMETHING FROM OUR DECISION."

Essex turned red with rage. He seemed at a loss for words and than all of a sudden he turned his back on her. This of course did not go unnoticed by Queen, who promptly smacked him across the face. Essex was so enraged that he jumped on his horse and galloped across the field. Queen just turned back to her councillor and finished her discussion.

Essex was not in the palace when we returned later that afternoon. He had gone to his own house. Later that week when someone remarked about it, Queen said, "Maybe he will return and maybe he won't"—as if she did not care.

When Essex came back to Court, the Queen took it calmly, acting as if nothing had happened and paying hardly any attention to him because she was paying so much attention to the war. The question of whom to send to Ireland which had still not been decided upon was once more brought up, and she held a great meeting to settle the matter.

I sneaked into the council room and hid under the table at which they were all sitting. Essex was also there. Once again he tried to show that he could get his way—and suggested that Carew be sent to Ireland. The Queen ignored his suggestion and made several of her own which were not ignored. Meanwhile I amused myself by jumping over all the noble feet.

Essex too had become restless. Finally he became so irritated, he cried, "In the name of God, Your Grace! I can fight better than any of these rogues in battle!"

I did not want to miss any part of what would happen next. I ventured out from my hiding place.

Queen looked disdainfully at Essex. "So Essex is brave enough to fight in battle. He is letting go of Queen's skirts."

A rumble of laughter filled the room.

Then she studied Essex seriously and turned to her council. "How about it, My Lords? Shall we send Essex to fight?" Her eyes went to each one of them with a look that was unmistakable.

Each quickly said, "Aye. Aye."

Queen glanced triumphantly at Essex. "You have won—for once."

I scurried under the table as Essex's noble feet carefully removed themselves and marched out of the room. Soon the other feet followed.

The door shut and I curled up and went to sleep in the darkness.

The following weeks were spent preparing for Essex's expedition to Ireland. Essex kept requesting supplies. Just as it would seem he had all he needed, he would ask for more. Finally he could no longer delay his departure. I watched from the balcony the day he and his men marched down the crowd-thronged streets of London toward the gates of the city.

Queen too watched Essex go. She scooped me up in her hands and petted me, murmuring to herself, "There goes a fool."

Finally he passed through the gates and was gone from sight.

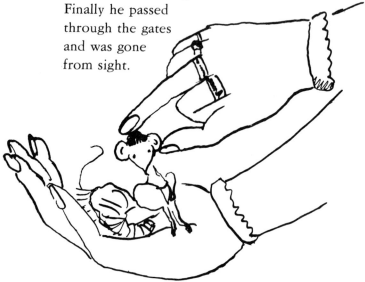

Essex was gone a long time. Queen kept sending letters, but Essex never returned any. He came back to England defeated. All of Queen's money had been wasted.

I don't exactly know what happened in Ireland, but I heard about how Essex tried to become King while he was there. Queen took away one of his titles, which made him less powerful. Then she ordered him imprisoned in his own house. A long time passed and she seemed to have forgotten him. She laughed and danced with her new favorites and lived her usual life. And then Essex grew very sick. Queen was frightened for his health. She wrote him kind letters which I found on her desk. I don't know if she ever sent them.

During Essex's siege of illness, Queen received a book about Henry IV who had killed his cousin to become King. (This book seemed to bother the Queen because she and Essex were very, very distantly related.) The book was dedicated to Essex! I heard Queen mumbling to herself one night as she read it. Suddenly she closed the book and threw it across the room. Next thing I learned of Essex was that all of his offices had been taken away. He had no more power—no more money.

The Queen then sent him a letter telling him that until her wishes were known he would remain imprisoned in his house. I wondered what Queen's wishes were, and while Essex and I and the rest of England waited, Queen seemed thoroughly wrapped up in arranging the wedding of one of her ladies-in-waiting. For weeks she worked on the plans for the wedding as if they meant the world to her. And Essex remained imprisoned. The wedding was celebrated and afterward Essex still seemed to be forgotten. And then I learned that Queen had had Essex released but ordered him to stay away from the Court.

One morning there was a great commotion in the palace. I was just about to venture into Queen's bedchamber through all the racket to see what was happening when Skidmore darted in and squeaked excitedly, "Attack! Attack!"

"What? Tell me!" I demanded of him. "Tell me!"

Skidmore breathlessly said, "An army, a big army, is coming to the palace!"

I was very frightened and Skidmore kept darting in and out of my hole with the latest news and going off to the Queen's balcony to get wind of any new developments.

Essex had evidently gone about London raising an army of men who did not want a Queen to rule them any longer. What I know now is that all that morning Essex had marched the streets, but that Queen, too clever for him, had closed some that led to the palace. While Essex was finding his way out of this maze, Queen sent some of her army to his house and ordered them to blow it up unless Essex surrendered.

Essex rushed to his house and threw down his sword when he saw that he was outnumbered. He was arrested and taken to the Tower, charged with treason. In addition, he was charged with all of the wrongs he had committed in Ireland. He was found guilty and sentenced to be beheaded.

On the day of Essex's execution, Skidmore was up bright and early. He arrived at my hole and begged me to go with him to the Tower.

I was shocked. "Skidmore, death is not fun. It is sad. Essex has been good to you and

now you are living it up upon his death. I'm ashamed of you!"

Skidmore looked thoughtful for a minute. "I'm mourning. I am going to watch him die and I'll mourn for him."

I looked at my friend and tears filled my eyes.

"There, there. Don't cry." Skidmore hugged me close.

"Thank you, Skidmore. It's just hard to know that he will die. Go along now. Don't watch too much, Skidmore. You'll have nightmares."

Skidmore nodded and was gone.

I went to Queen's study, where she had buried herself in a Latin history book. She looked at me and smiled weakly. "His time has come," was all she said. She picked me up. She looked tired. I curled up in her hand. We sat together for a long time. And then the drums rolled and the cannons boomed.

Queen dropped me. She rushed to her bed chamber and slammed the door. Sadly I returned to my hole.

Skidmore came in late that night. He sat on my bed and told me that he was scared. "You can sleep here tonight," I said.

Skidmore said, "I have to tell you about it to get it off my mind." And he told me it all, and then he went to sleep.

But I was awake all night jumping at the slightest shadow. Early next morning, when I at last fell into a troubled slumber, I dreamed of the execution. I saw everything Skidmore had told me.

I dreamed of Essex walking to the block wearing a black coat and hat. I saw him remove his hat and address the lords who were there to witness his death. He talked for a long time about all the things he had done wrong. Then he prayed, asking God to forgive his enemies and prayed for our Queen. Then he took off his cloak and ruff. He was wearing a black doublet.

He knelt down by the block and prayed some more.

The man who was to behead him asked Essex's forgiveness for what he was about to do. And Essex forgave him. Then he stood up and removed his black doublet. Underneath that he was wearing a scarlet waistcoat with long scarlet sleeves. He looked magnificent. He turned and bowed and said he would signal them of his readiness to die by stretching out his arms. He lay down flat on the scaffold, turned his head sideways, and threw his arms out.

The axe swung up and met its destination with a loud whack. Two more times did it strike before Essex's head rolled in the straw. The executioner picked up Essex's head and showed it to the lords saying ''God save the Queen!''

I woke with a start.

Chapter
9

WHEN I OPENED MY EYES the morning after, there was a sense of something missing. The day was gray and rainy. My room was freezing cold and I felt strangely lonely. It was altogether not a morning to get out of bed, so I didn't. Just as I was resettling myself I thought of Queen. I wanted to find out just how she had taken it. Queen was not in her bedchamber and not in her study. I scurried along the passageways until I came to the balcony. There was Queen all in blue, sneezing into a handkerchief. I wondered why she was out on such a miserable day. A lady-in-waiting suddenly appeared and said, "Your Grace, have you not had your breath of air yet?"

"Yes, Catherine, you may help me back now," was the prim reply.

I scampered along after them. Queen was led to her bedchamber. Here she sank onto her bed. The lady-in-waiting went about neatening the room and closing the thick draperies which hung in folds to the floor and which I often loved to slide down. Then the lady curtsied and Queen waved her away with her hand. She fell into a slumber murmuring "Essex" in her dreams.

The days dragged by and all went gloomily from drab to dull. There were but a few fleeting moments of laughter and dance, then dull to drab once more.

A year passed. Queen was seventy and became restless and old overnight, it seemed to me. I watched her sink onto some pillows and heard her sigh. It was a long, sad sigh as the one you might make if you had a purse of money and spent it all at once on the wrong thing. It was then that I realized what her seventieth year meant. She was old and frail and sad and dull.

And Queen was dying. I was the first to realize it.

Queen spent most of that year on the floor on pillows with a sword by her side. She threw fits and tantrums, ate little, hardly slept, wouldn't drink, refused comfort except for music, and would lie for hours staring at the floor with one finger in her mouth. On one occasion she lay on the floor and suddenly screamed, "ESSEX" and started thrusting the sword into the tapestries on the wall. She reminded me somewhat of the lord's wife in the play by Shakespeare which he presented at the Court a happier time ago. Sometimes she fell down on her pillows and cried.

She repeated this performance many times on different days and took to crying quite frequently. She seemed ruined spiritually. Then the New Year of 1603 came and she seemed lighter. On January 14, a doctor said she had a bad cold and suggested that the Court move to Richmond, which is a warmer palace—less drafty. Skidmore and I hid in the Queen's carriage and I nestled in her hair. She lifted a weak hand and stroked me. I shall never forget it. We arrived at

Richmond and Queen was helped to her chambers. She seemed very tired and unhappy.

Many people came to visit her during the next few weeks. But Queen seemed lifeless and disinterested. I spent much time with her during the last days of her life and once when she collapsed and cried, I clambered up to her face and licked away her tears to show her that I was still there.

On March 23, her secretary came, and seeing her dying face said, "Scotland?" to which she painfully nodded. I understood that James of Scotland would next be King. And then the Archbishop of Canterbury stepped forward and prayed at her bedside. He prayed for a long, long time and then he turned to rise, but Queen seemed to have taken a pleasure in his prayers and pushed him down again. For another long time he prayed but still was not allowed to leave.

I was getting drowsy and wanted to curl up and sleep, but Queen was the one whom I felt responsible for and so I watched over her again. It was not till late at night that he left and only because Queen was asleep. And so gratefully I curled up upon her hair, licking her cheek as I did.

I do not know when during the night her heart ceased to beat. I do not know when the greatest queen England ever had seen died. All I know is that when I opened my eyes the next morning her cheek was cold and stiff. I nestled into her hair and cried and cried. Queen was dead and although I'd known it was coming, I could never feel as I did in that one fleeting moment when I kissed her cheek and knew she

was gone. My only Queen who was more beloved to me than anything else had died. I moved
to my nest under her bed. And I cried myself to
sleep.

And here I close my memoir. For after her
death nothing else is worth recording anymore.
May this memoir be as beloved as my Queen
was.

Esther closed the book. She put her paw to her face to wipe away the tears. "Well, I do declare! This book has kept me reading for hours."

She thought about her illustrious past. Then she rose and swept into the kitchen trying to act the way a mouse with a royal past would. The way Elizabeth did. "I shall fix myself some supper." And as she was eating it she thought of what Madame Wimble had said.

"If I am related to royalty then I must be of a higher class than Madame Wimble." The thought pleased her.

"From now on I will act, look, and live the way a mouse of my station should." And so saying she pulled out all the plushy bits and decorated her house with them. Then she gracefully sank down onto her favorite armchair. "Goodness, it must be late—and to act and look like a mouse of royalty I shall have to have enough sleep." And with that she swept into her bedroom.

The next morning Esther went around her house examining everything. "This will simply not do. I am a mouse of royalty," she thought. "I ought to be living where royalty lives."

And so that is why later that afternoon Esther, pulling a tiny cartload of furniture and belongings, waved good-bye to her friends and the house at Plum Pit Grove and left to move into Buckingham Palace. Some of the mice helped her along the inside passages to the doorway and along the street. At the palace gates they left her and she slipped easily between the bars and into a small hole in the stone wall of the palace. "It is very convenient, this hole, and must mean other mice live here," she told herself.

She worked her way through a series of difficult passages. Then she found the Branch of the Bedroom off one of the passageways. She found a small vacant hole and dumped all of her belongings onto the floor.

In a few days Esther was all settled in her new home. She spread her plush on the floor and set up her furniture. And then she made a lovely discovery. The Queen occupying the Palace was Elizabeth II. How fitting!